A NOTE TO PARENTS

When your children are ready to "step into reading," giving them the right books is as crucial as giving them the right food to eat. **Step into Reading Books** present exciting stories and information reinforced with lively, colorful illustrations that make learning to read fun, satisfying, and worthwhile. They are priced so that acquiring an entire library of them is affordable. And they are beginning readers with a difference—they're written on five levels.

Early Step into Reading Books are designed for brand-new readers, with large type and only one or two lines of very simple text per page. **Step 1 Books** feature the same easy-to-read type as the Early Step into Reading Books, but with more words per page. **Step 2 Books** are both longer and slightly more difficult, while **Step 3 Books** introduce readers to paragraphs and fully developed plot lines. **Step 4 Books** offer exciting nonfiction for the increasingly independent reader.

The grade levels assigned to the five steps—preschool through kindergarten for the Early Books, preschool through grade 1 for Step 1, grades 1 through 3 for Step 2, grades 2 through 3 for Step 3, and grades 2 through 4 for Step 4—are intended only as guides. Some children move through all five steps very rapidly; others climb the steps over a period of several years. Either way, these books will help your child "step into reading" in style!

For Artemis and her snow day friends
Shira, Sarah, Laura, Melissa and for my
snow day friend Barbara Carey.

Text copyright © 1998 by Corinne Demas Bliss
Illustrations copyright © 1998 by Nancy Poydar
All rights reserved under International and Pan-American Copyright Conventions.
Published in the United States by Random House, Inc., New York, and simultaneously
in Canada by Random House of Canada Limited, Toronto.

www.randomhouse.com/kids/

Library of Congress Cataloging-in-Publication Data
Bliss, Corinne Demas.
Snow day / by Corinne Demas Bliss ; illustrated by Nancy Poydar.
    p.   cm. — (Step into reading. A step 2 book)
SUMMARY: When school is canceled because of snow, Emily not only has fun playing
outside with her friends but she also finally decides on a topic for her class report.
ISBN 0-679-88222-7 (pbk.). — ISBN 0-679-98222-1 (lib. bdg.)
[1. Snow—Fiction.   2. Schools—Fiction.]   I. Poydar, Nancy, ill.   II. Title.   III. Series:
Step into reading.   Step 2 book.
PZ7.B61917Sn   1998   [E]—dc21   97-45810

Printed in the United States of America   10 9 8 7 6 5 4 3 2 1

STEP INTO READING is a registered trademark of Random House, Inc.

Step into Reading®

Snow Day

by Corinne Demas Bliss
illustrated by Nancy Poydar

A Step 2 Book

Random House New York

4

It was snowing!

Emily looked out the window.

Maybe there would be

a snow day tomorrow.

"How are you coming along
with your report topics, class?"
asked Ms. Dever.

Emily looked at the books on her desk.
She still didn't know what
to write her report about.
If there was a snow day,
she would have an extra day
to think of a topic.

Maybe it would snow

for two days.

Then she wouldn't have to find

a topic till next week.

Maybe it would snow so much

they'd call off school

for the whole year.

Then she'd *never* have to do a report.

Emily looked over
at her friend Marietta.
Marietta was the new girl in class.

Marietta already had a great topic: volcanoes.

Emily wished she'd thought of it first.

At the end of school, the kids were
a little wild in the coat room.
"Bet we have a snow day tomorrow!"
said Brian.
"Snow day?" asked Marietta.

"Don't you know what
  a snow day is?" asked Brian.
"Of course I do," said Marietta.
"Where I come from,
  we had snow days all the time."

"I didn't know they had snow
in California," said Emily.
"California is a very big state,"
said Marietta.
"They have everything in
California."

"Want to come over tomorrow
if it's a snow day?" asked Emily.
"Sure," said Marietta.
Marietta's backpack had
a dozen patches sewn on it.
Now all the kids wanted patches
on their backpacks, too.

Emily walked home.

She loved the snow.

The snowflakes were fat and lazy.

Emily stuck out her tongue

and caught a snowflake on the tip.

Wham! A big snowball hit Emily
on her bare neck.
Her skin stung.
Icy snow slid down
inside her collar.

She looked around.

Brian had been hiding

behind a tree.

"Gotcha!" he cried.

Emily ran into her house.
She had forgotten about
the big problem with snow:
snowballs.

The next morning,

Emily's mother called upstairs,

"Snow day!"

"Hurray!" shouted Emily.

"No school!"

She wouldn't have to worry about
her report topic until tomorrow.

Emily's brothers were eating breakfast.
"Brian's coming over,"
said her big brother.
"We're going to have
a big snowball fight!"

Emily pulled up the collar
of her bathrobe.

"Marietta is coming over," she said.

"We're going to play inside."

"Inside?" asked Emily's mother.
"Won't Marietta want to play
  in the snow?"
"Where Marietta comes from,
  they had snow days all the time,"
  said Emily.

"I thought she came from
California," said Emily's mother.
"California is a very big state,"
said Emily.
"They have everything in
California."

When Marietta came over,
Brian and Emily's brothers
were in the backyard
building a snow fort.
They had a big pile of snowballs
ready for battle.

"I thought we'd play inside,"
said Emily.

"Inside?" asked Marietta. "Why?"

"You must be tired of playing in the
snow," said Emily, "since you had it all
the time where you came from."

Marietta got a funny look
on her face.
"If I tell you a secret," she said,
"will you promise not to tell anyone?"
Emily nodded.
"I come from the part of California
where there isn't any snow,"
said Marietta.
"I've never played in it before.
So I'd really like to play outside."

"You never had a snow day before?"
asked Emily.

"No," said Marietta.

"But I didn't want everyone to know."

"If *I* tell *you* a secret,

will you promise not to tell?"

asked Emily.

"Okay," said Marietta.

"The real reason I don't want

to play outside," said Emily,

"is because the boys will throw

snowballs at us."

"Oh," said Marietta.

"Well, I don't intend to put up with *that!*"

Emily followed Marietta outside.

Emily ducked when the first snowball

came her way.

Marietta walked right up

to the snow fort.

The snowballs stopped.

"What's this supposed to be?"
she asked.
"Haven't you ever seen
a snow fort before?" asked Brian.

"Of course I have," said Marietta.

"Where I come from,

all the little kids make snow forts."

"Little kids?" asked Brian.

"What do the big kids make?"

"Snow towns," said Marietta.

"How do you make a snow town?"
asked Emily's big brother.
"First you make a main street,"
said Marietta. "Then you make
the stores, the school, and the bank
with snow money."

"I'll make the bank," said Emily's
big brother.
"I want to make the bank, too!"
said Emily's little brother.
"You can make the post office,"
said Emily, "and snow packages."

Brian made a restaurant

full of snow food.

Emily made a bakery

full of snow cakes and snow pies.

Some other kids wanted to join in.

"There's one rule," said Marietta.

"This is a peaceful town.

No snowballs allowed."

"Can't I serve spaghetti and snowballs
in my restaurant?" asked Brian.
Marietta looked at Emily.
"That kind of snowball is okay
with me," said Emily,
and they all laughed.

Soon all the kids

were working on the town.

There was a library

filled with snow books

and a supermarket that sold

snowcream, snowbeans, snowfish,

snowpolish, and snowsuds.

Emily whispered to Marietta.

"If you never played in snow before,

how did you know about snow towns?"

"Oh, I just made it up,"

said Marietta, smiling.

"It's great," said Emily.

"I wish it could stay cold forever
 and the town would never melt."

"Melt!" cried Marietta.

"I forgot about that.
 What do we do then?"

"Wait for the next snow day,"
 said Emily, "and build a new town."

That night before she went to bed,
Emily looked out at the snow town.
It was snowing again.
Emily reached out the window
and caught a snowflake
on her finger.

Was it true that all snowflakes

had six sides?

Was it true that no two snowflakes

were exactly alike?

Emily knew more about snow

than Marietta, but there was still

a lot to learn.

Emily smiled.

Now she wasn't worried about

finding a topic for her report.

It was right there, outside

her window.

She'd tell Ms. Dever about it

at school tomorrow.

Unless, of course,

it was another snow day.